My inspiration and support come from many sources but thank you to my loving partner Andrew, my two amazing children, and my Mom. Without you all pushing me to finish this project, I would have never believed it could be done!

Publishing Co.: Pink Helmet Publishing
ISBN #: 978-17752444

Hi, I'm Zippy the turtle!

Psst... down here

*T*his is a story about my friend Claire…
and how she got her pink helmet.

When Claire was born, her mom and dad noticed her head wasn't growing as it should. They went to see the doctor.

*T*he doctor measured her head and it did not seem as round as it should be!

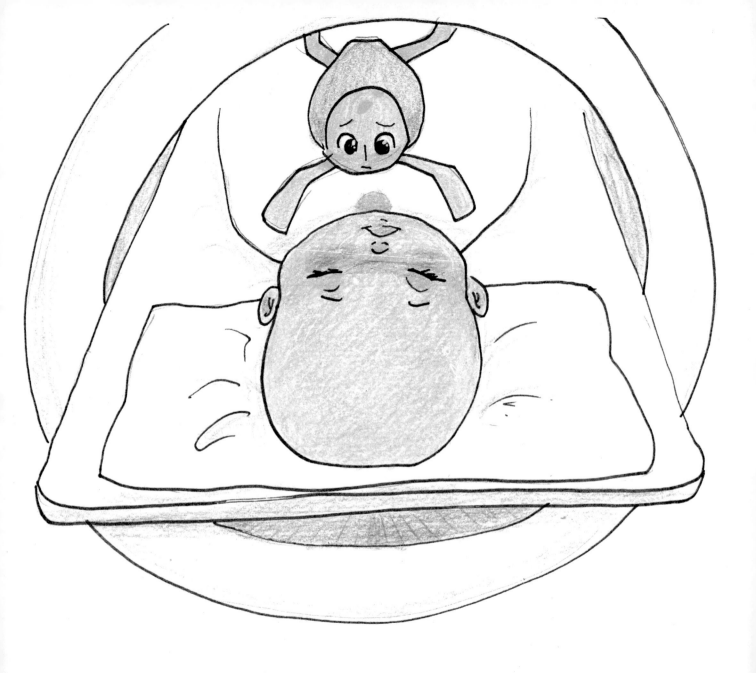

She had to get a picture of her skull, that is the part of the head that protects your brain. It is like the shell on my back and how it protects my body!

An X-ray machine took the picture of Claire's skull, she was nervous. I held her hand so she would be still, we imagined it was a robot reading our minds.

The doctor told Claire she had to have an operation that would help her head grow properly and make room for her brain! It would be the first operation of its kind done at the children's hospital. This was very exciting for the doctors; learning on Claire meant they could help other kids like her.

Claire's Mum and Dad were very scared!!!

So Claire had to be brave.

This is where I, Zippy, was able to help. I stayed with Claire the whole time, making sure she would be ok!

The only time she cried was when they told her she was not allowed to eat before the operation. Eating was Claire's favourite thing to do!

Now it was time for surgery...

*T*he nurse gave Claire a little pink hospital gown with white stripes. She kissed her Mum and Dad goodbye. Her Mum whispered her favourite song softly in her ear...

"All my lovin' I will send to you..."

Then off we went, through two big swinging doors and down a long hallway. Claire and I were feeling nervous now...

*I*n the operating room, the doctors and nurses sang and danced about. They wore really cool costumes, like superheroes, with masks and hats and gowns that looked like capes. We did not want to tell them their capes were on backwards.

We even did some counting...the nurse asked us to count to 5

"1...2....3... ..."

*C*laire was fast asleep. She had the most wonderful nap while the doctors operated on her head!

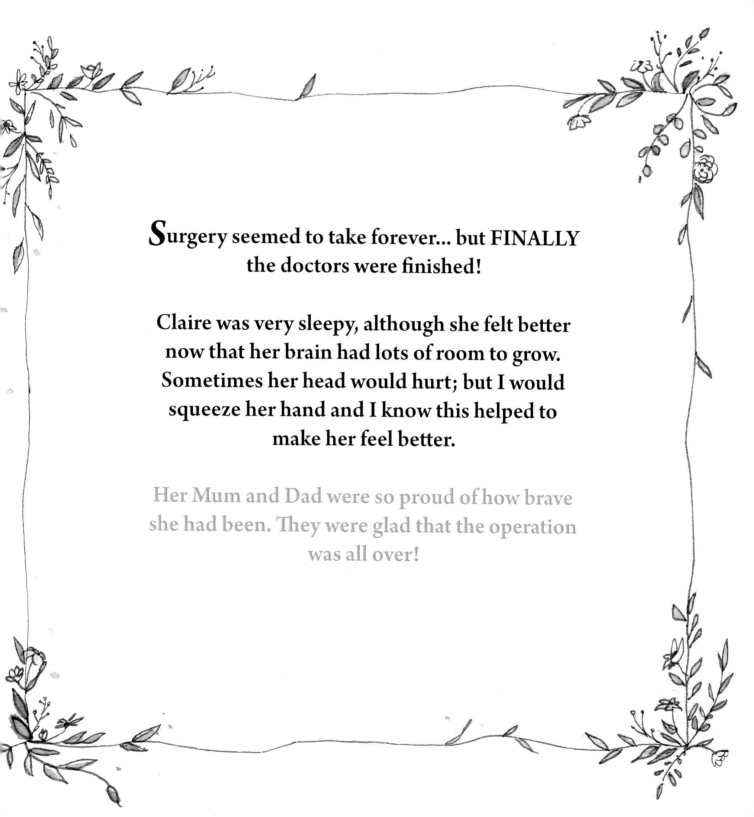

Surgery seemed to take forever... but FINALLY the doctors were finished!

Claire was very sleepy, although she felt better now that her brain had lots of room to grow. Sometimes her head would hurt; but I would squeeze her hand and I know this helped to make her feel better.

Her Mum and Dad were so proud of how brave she had been. They were glad that the operation was all over!

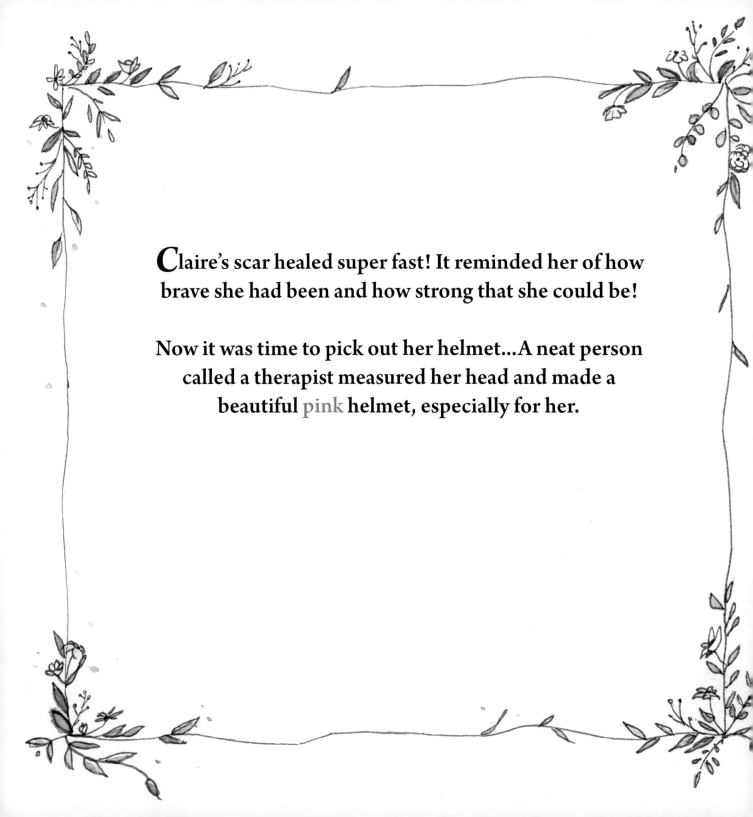

Claire's scar healed super fast! It reminded her of how brave she had been and how strong that she could be!

Now it was time to pick out her helmet...A neat person called a therapist measured her head and made a beautiful pink helmet, especially for her.

At first, her pink helmet was hard to get use to... always making her head sweaty and making her lose balance. Eventually, like my shell, it became a special part of her.

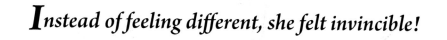

Instead of feeling different, she felt invincible!

She had to wear the helmet all the time so that her head would grow into its round shape.
Now, she did not have to worry about bumping her head or falling down. She thought

'Why don't all kids wear helmets!?'

*E*verywhere Claire would go, she told the people she met about her helmet and our adventure to the hospital. She made lots of new friends and became known as 'The Girl in the Pink Helmet'.

Claire was so thankful to all the people that took care of her during her surgery and recovery. Her Mum and Dad, family and friends, the doctors, nurses and therapists and of course all the people she met along the way!

*B*eing sick is NOT fun… but when you have loved ones to hold your hand and special people to care for you along the way… you can make it through anything!!

- Zippy

Ange Denny spent her years growing up on islands, from Campobello Island to Prince Edward Island and now Vancouver Island. She loved to write in journals about anything and everything. When it became time to choose a career, these things were tucked away and her education took the forefront. She graduated with a degree in Psychology and Biology and not long after, her Bachelor in Nursing. She now lives in Victoria, B.C. working as a RN. Ange is rekindling her love for writing as she balances work and raising

her two children. She finds her inspiration and support in her partner Andrew and two young children, Claire and Malcolm.

Claire Bell was welcomed into the world in Prince Rupert, B.C. by awestruck parents, Ange and Andrew. Claire overwhelmed their home with joy. From early on, they knew she would do amazing things. Ange and Andrew understood that parenting would be a challenge; little did they realize the emotional journey that would entail. Claire was diagnosed with Left Coronal Synostosis at 2 months old and underwent cranial surgery at 3 months old. It was the first endoscopic craniosynostosis repair surgery performed at BC Children's Hospital in Vancouver, B.C. It was a great success! After healing, Claire was fitted for a pink orthotic helmet. She wore it for the next 8 months to assist with the re-molding of her skull. Now, three years later, Claire carries on as any toddler would; with no limitations to brain growth or cognitive development. She is a beautiful, compassionate little girl with a tiny scar on her head and a pretty pink helmet on her dresser to remind her of her experience. Claire enjoys princess dresses', dancing, coloring and reading. Of course, her Daddy and brother Malcolm are her biggest fans!

Made in the USA
San Bernardino, CA
27 October 2018